# Dear Parent:

Congratulations! Your child is taking
the first steps on an exciting journey.
The destination? Independent reading!

**STEP INTO READING®** will help your child get there. The program offers
five steps to reading success. Each step includes fun stories and colorful art.
There are also Step into Reading Sticker Books, Step into Reading Math
Readers, Step into Reading Phonics Readers, Step into Reading Write-In
Readers, and Step into Reading Phonics Boxed Sets—a complete literacy
program with something to interest every child.

## Learning to Read, Step by Step!

**Ready to Read   Preschool–Kindergarten**
• big type and easy words • rhyme and rhythm • picture clues
For children who know the alphabet and are eager to
begin reading.

**Reading with Help   Preschool–Grade 1**
• basic vocabulary • short sentences • simple stories
For children who recognize familiar words and sound out
new words with help.

**Reading on Your Own   Grades 1–3**
• engaging characters • easy-to-follow plots • popular topics
For children who are ready to read on their own.

**Reading Paragraphs   Grades 2–3**
• challenging vocabulary • short paragraphs • exciting stories
For newly independent readers who read simple sentences
with confidence.

**Ready for Chapters   Grades 2–4**
• chapters • longer paragraphs • full-color art
For children who want to take the plunge into chapter books
but still like colorful pictures.

**STEP INTO READING®** is designed to give every child a successful
reading experience. The grade levels are only guides. Children can progress
through the steps at their own speed, developing confidence in their
reading, no matter what their grade.

Remember, a lifetime love of reading starts with a single step!

For my mom, with love.

—A.J.

Visit us on the Web!
StepIntoReading.com
www.randomhouse.com/kids
Educators and librarians, for a variety of teaching tools, visit us at www.randomhouse.com/teachers

ISBN: 978-0-7364-2777-7 (trade)
ISBN: 978-0-7364-8092-5 (lib. bdg.)

Printed in the United States of America     10  9  8  7  6  5  4  3  2

DISNEP · PIXAR

**TOY STORY**

# A Spooky Adventure

By Apple Jordan

Illustrated by Alan Batson and Lori Tyminski

Random House 🏠 New York

Woody and his friends loved their new home. Bonnie loved to play with her new toys.

Bonnie's favorite game
was Bakery.
But her bakery
was spooky!

One rainy day,
Bonnie and her family
went out.
Her toys were home alone.

Outside,
thunder boomed.
Lightning flashed
in the sky.

The Potato Heads
jumped.
Bullseye hid
in a drawer.

Slinky peeked
out the window.
Rex said the house
was haunted!

Jessie hugged Bullseye.
Buzz turned
on his laser light.
Woody said the house
was not haunted.

Bonnie's old toys
would show
their new friends.

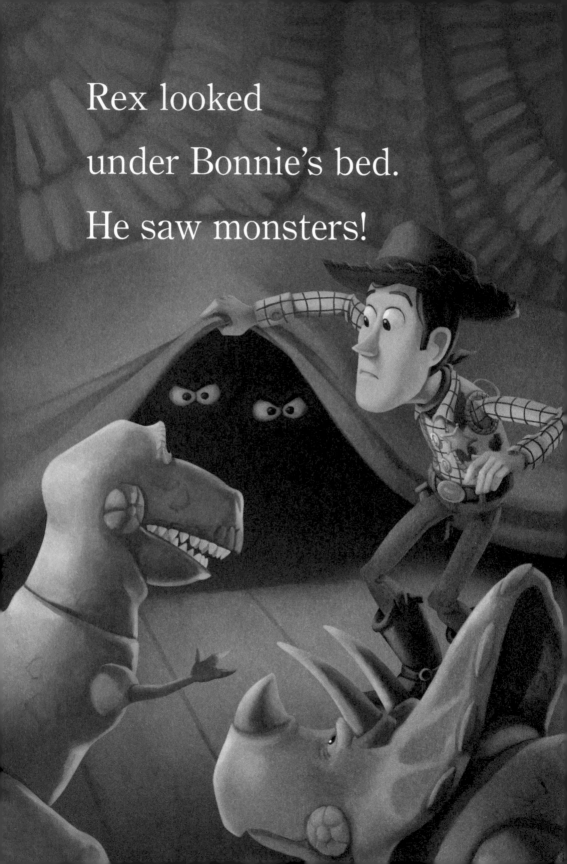

Rex looked
under Bonnie's bed.
He saw monsters!

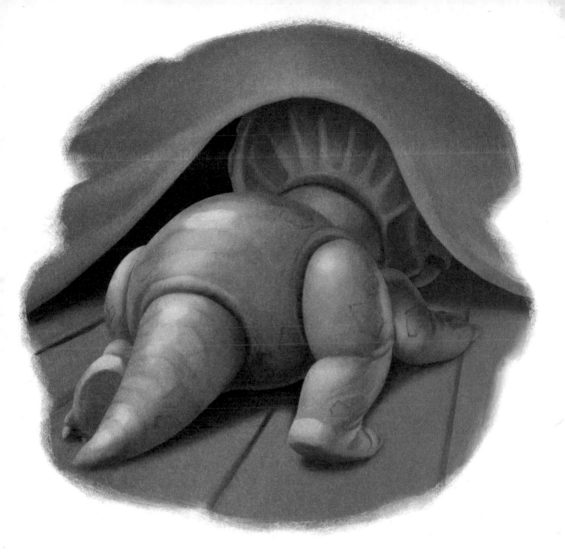

But Trixie said
there were no monsters.
She crawled
under the bed.

Trixie showed Rex the monsters. They were Bonnie's bunny slippers!

The toys
heard scratching
at the window.
Bullseye hid
behind Woody.
Was it a ghost?

Buttercup opened
the curtain.

It was not a ghost!
Bonnie's kite was stuck
in the tree.

Soon the toys
heard a spooky sound.
<u>Hooo! Hooo! Hooo!</u>

Hamm said it
was a goblin.

Buzz and Woody
led the gang
down the hall.

Mr. Pricklepants
opened the blinds.
The sound was
not a goblin.
It was just an owl!

Thud!

The toys heard a sound
from the kitchen.

The toys went
to the kitchen.
Chuckles told them
to watch out.

But Woody was
not worried.

Chuckles opened
the closet door.
Woody froze.
Buzz jumped.
Rex yelled.

There was a dragon
in the closet!

Chuckles turned
on the light.

It was not a dragon!
It was just an old mop.

The toys all laughed.

There were no monsters.

There were no ghosts.

There were no goblins.

There were no dragons.

Bonnie's house
was not haunted.

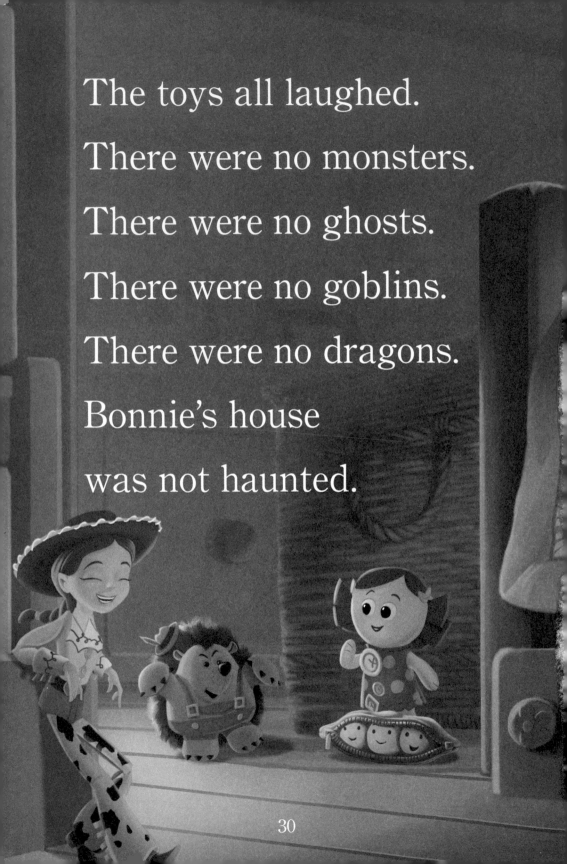

But sometimes it was still a little spooky.